BEAR IN A SQUARE

Written by Stella Blackstone
Illustrated by Debbie Harter

Barefoot Books
Celebrating Art and Story

www.barefootbooks.com

Find the bear
in the square

Find the hearts
in the queen's hair

Find the circles
in the pool

Find the rectangles in the school

Find the moons in the cave

Find the triangles on the wave

Find the diamonds on the crown

Find the zigzags around the clown

Find the ovals
in the park

Find the stars
in the dark

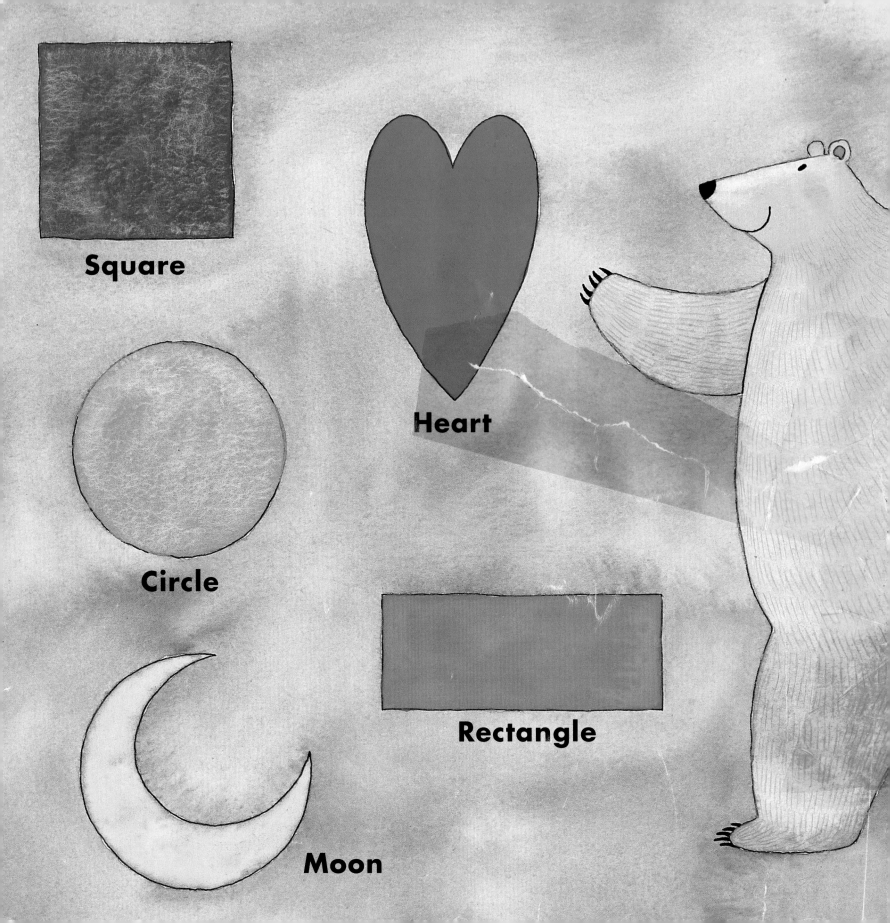

Square

Heart

Circle

Rectangle

Moon

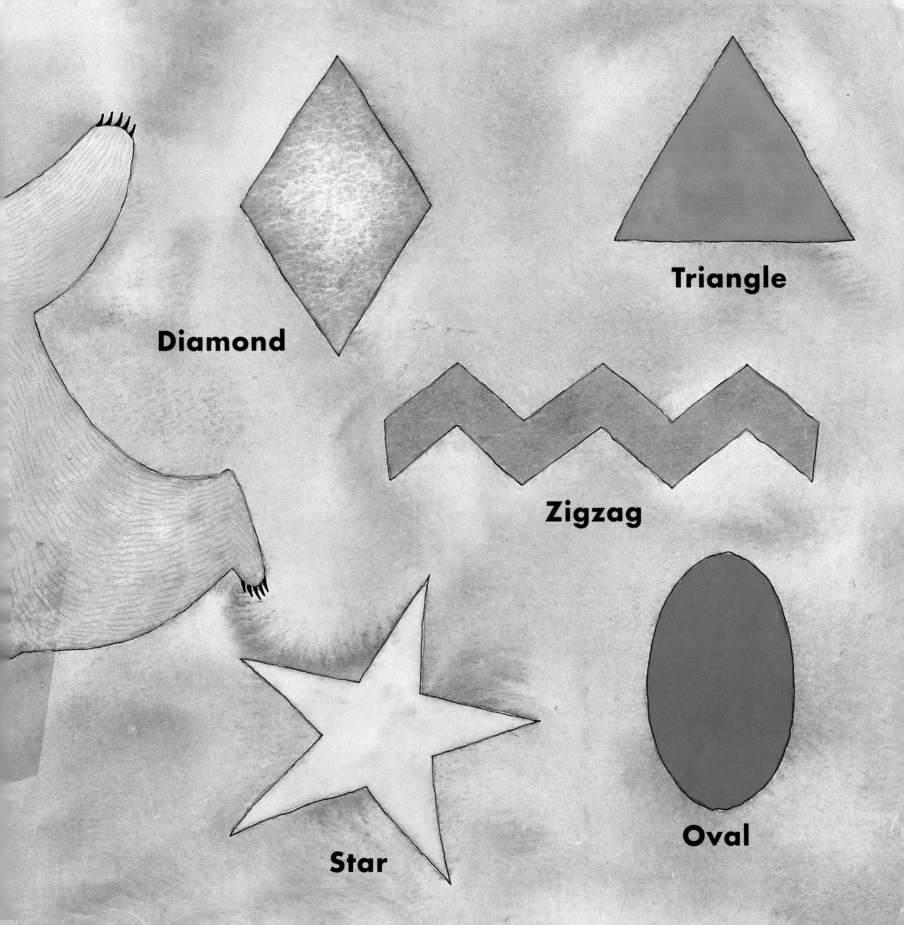

Diamond

Triangle

Zigzag

Star

Oval

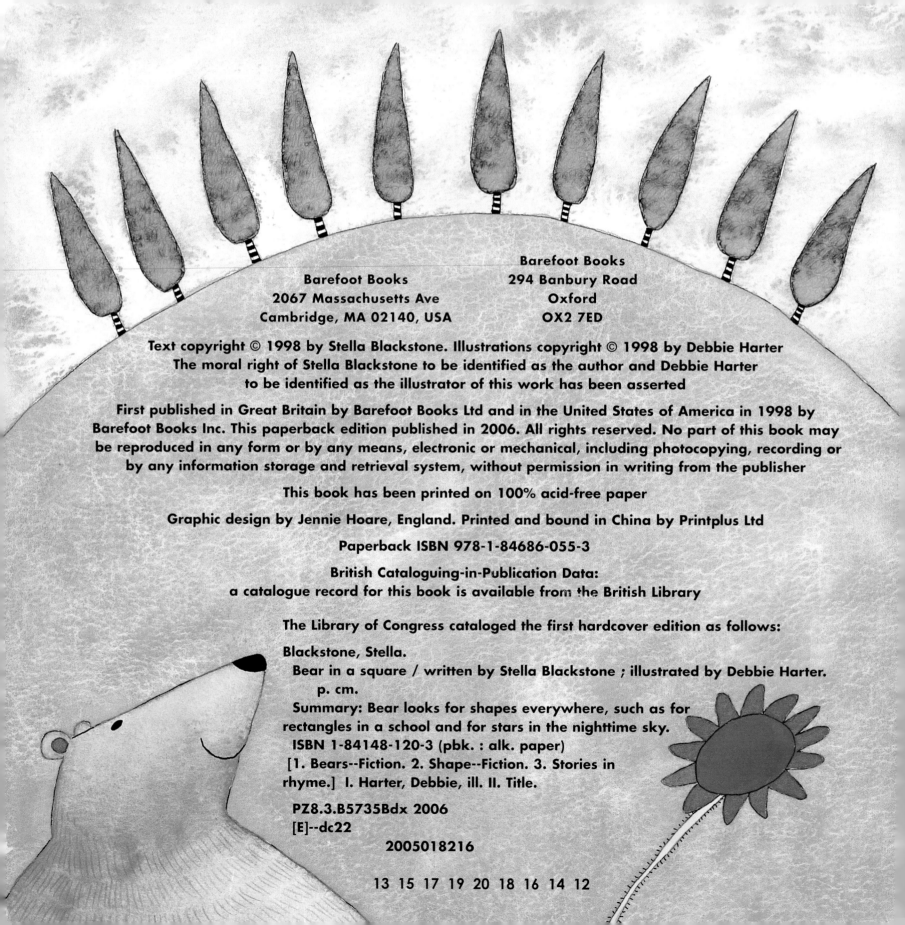

Barefoot Books
2067 Massachusetts Ave
Cambridge, MA 02140, USA

Barefoot Books
294 Banbury Road
Oxford
OX2 7ED

This book has been printed on 100% acid-free paper

Graphic design by Jennie Hoare, England. Printed and bound in China by Printplus Ltd

Paperback ISBN 978-1-84686-055-3

British Cataloguing-in-Publication Data:
a catalogue record for this book is available from the British Library

The Library of Congress cataloged the first hardcover edition as follows:

Blackstone, Stella.
  Bear in a square / written by Stella Blackstone ; illustrated by Debbie Harter.
     p. cm.
  Summary: Bear looks for shapes everywhere, such as for
rectangles in a school and for stars in the nighttime sky.
  ISBN 1-84148-120-3 (pbk. : alk. paper)
  [1. Bears--Fiction. 2. Shape--Fiction. 3. Stories in
rhyme.] I. Harter, Debbie, ill. II. Title.

PZ8.3.B5735Bdx 2006
[E]--dc22

                2005018216

          13 15 17 19 20 18 16 14 12